The Pea

To my mum Fathé, my princess in heaven.

First published in the UK in 2017
by New Frontier Publishing Pty Ltd
93 Harbord Street, London SW6 6PN
www.newfrontierpublishing.co.uk

ISBN: 978-1-912076-60-4 (PB)

A CIP catalogue record for this book is available from
the British Library.

Designed by Celeste Hulme

Printed in China
10 9 8 7 6 5 4 3 2 1

Happily Ever After

The Princess and the Pea

Illustrated by Helene Magisson

NEW FRONTIER PUBLISHING

A long time ago a prince wanted to marry a princess.

The prince searched far and wide for a real princess.

He went to London but the princess drank tea
from a mug.

Italian Tea

English Tea

Russian Tea

Indian Tea

Chinese Tea

French Tea

Australian Tea

Japanese Tea

He went to Paris but the princess knew
nothing about art.

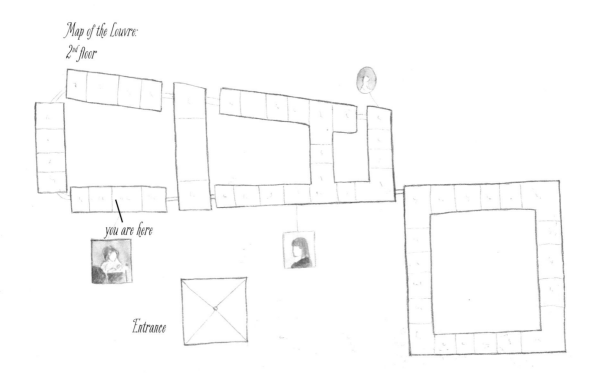

Map of the Louvre:
2nd floor

you are here

Entrance

He went to Italy but the princess slurped
her spaghetti.

The prince arrived home very sad indeed.
He just didn't know where he would find the
perfect princess.

Then one night there was a terrible storm. Thunder cracked loudly and lightning lit up the sky. Rain poured down the sides of the great palace.

Suddenly there was a knock at the door. When the king opened the door he saw before him a princess. But what a sight she was! Her long hair was soaking wet from the rain and her shoes were full of water.

The queen took one look at this princess and exclaimed, 'We will soon see if she is a *real* princess!'

The prince made the princess a cup of hot chocolate and handed her a towel to dry her hair. The princess thought he was quite the handsomest prince she had ever seen.

The queen crept off to the bedroom. She took twenty mattresses and laid them on a pea, then placed twenty blankets between the mattresses.

The bed was now ready for the princess.

Even though the princess was very tired,
she tossed and turned all night, unable
to sleep.

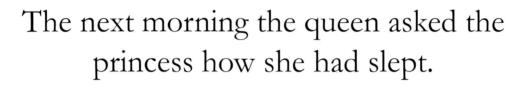

The next morning the queen asked the princess how she had slept.

'Oh, very badly indeed. There was something terribly hard under my bed,' replied the princess.

Now the queen knew that she was a real princess. Only a princess would have felt a pea through twenty mattresses and twenty blankets.

The prince was very happy as he rather liked the princess. The king and queen busied themselves organising the wedding.

On the day of their wedding, all the guests
shared a very special wedding cake.

The prince and princess lived happily
ever after.